The
Frog Prince
CONTINUED

STORY BY JON SCIESZKA

PAINTINGS BY STEVE JOHNSON

PUFFIN BOOKS

PUFFIN BOOKS
Published by the Penguin Group
Penguin Books USA Inc., 375 Hudson Street, New York, New York 10014, U.S.A.
Penguin Books Ltd, 27 Wrights Lane, London W8 5TZ, England
Penguin Books Australia Ltd, Ringwood, Victoria, Australia
Penguin Books Canada Ltd, 10 Alcorn Avenue, Toronto, Ontario, Canada M4V 3B2
Penguin Books (N.Z.) Ltd, 182-190 Wairau Road, Auckland 10, New Zealand

Penguin Books Ltd, Registered Offices: Harmondsworth, Middlesex, England

First published in the United States of America by Viking Penguin,
a division of Penguin Books USA Inc., 1991
Published in Puffin Books, 1994

1 3 5 7 9 10 8 6 4 2

THE LIBRARY OF CONGRESS HAS CATALOGED THE VIKING EDITION AS FOLLOWS:
Scieszka, Jon.
The Frog Prince, Continued / by Jon Scieszka; illustrated by Steve Johnson.   p.   cm.
Summary: After the frog turns into a prince, he and the princess do not
live happily ever after and the Prince decides to look
for a witch to help him remedy the situation.
ISBN 0-670-83421-1
[1. Fairy tales. 2. Princes—Fiction.] I. Johnson, Steve, ill. II. Title.
PZ7.S3134Fr   1991   [E]—dc20   90-26537   CIP   AC

Puffin Books ISBN 0-14-054285-X

Printed in United States of America
Set in Caledonia

Book design and art direction by Lou Fancher with Jeri Hansen.

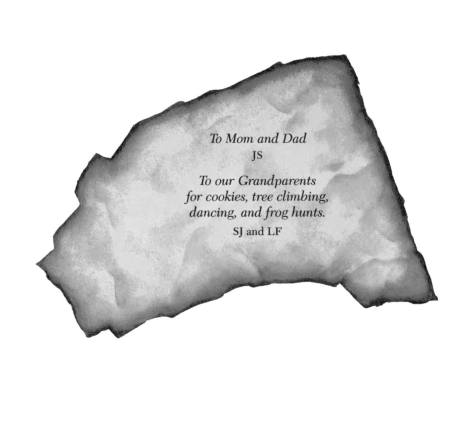

To Mom and Dad
JS

To our Grandparents
for cookies, tree climbing,
dancing, and frog hunts.
SJ and LF

The Princess kissed the frog.
He turned into a prince.
And they lived happily ever after...

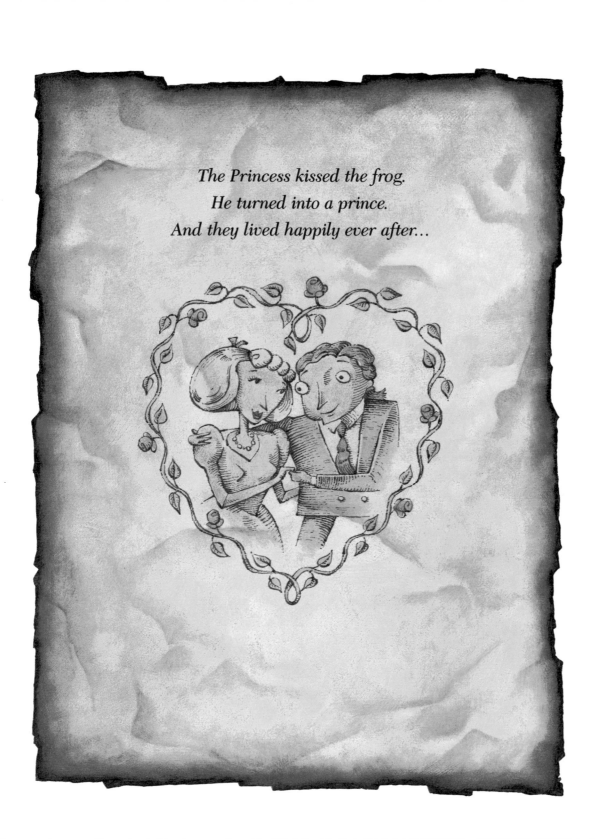

Well, let's just say they lived sort of happily for a long time.

Okay, so they weren't so happy.

In fact, they were miserable.

"Stop sticking your tongue out like that," nagged the Princess.

"How come you never want to go down to the pond anymore?" whined the Prince.

The Prince and Princess were so unhappy. They didn't know what to do.

"I would prefer that you not hop around on the furniture," said the Princess. "And it might be nice if you got out of the castle once in a while to slay a dragon or giant or whatever."

The Prince didn't feel like going out and slaying anything.
He just felt like running away. But then he reread
his book. And it said right there at the end of his story:
"They lived happily ever after. The End."
So he stayed in the castle and drove the Princess crazy.

Then one day, the Princess threw a perfectly
awful fit.

"First you keep me awake all night with your
horrible, croaking snore. Now I find a lily pad in your
pocket. I can't believe I actually kissed your slimy
frog lips. Sometimes I think we would both be better
off if you were still a frog."

That's when the idea hit him.

The Prince thought. "Still a frog. . . .Yes! That's it!"
And he ran off into the forest, looking for a witch
who could turn him back into a frog.

The Prince hadn't gone far when he ran into just
the person he was looking for.

"Miss Witch, Miss Witch. Excuse me, Miss Witch.
I wonder if you could help me?"

"Say, you're not looking for a princess to kiss
are you?" asked the witch.

"Oh, no. I've already been kissed. I'm the
Frog Prince. Actually, I was hoping you could turn
me back into a frog."

"Are you sure you're not looking for a beautiful
sleeping princess to kiss and wake up?"

"No, no—I'm the Frog Prince."

"That's funny. You don't look like a frog.
Well, no matter. If you're a prince, you're a prince.
And I'll have to cast a nasty spell on you.
I can't have any princes waking up Sleeping Beauty
before the hundred years are up."

The Prince didn't stick around to see which nasty
spell the witch had in mind. He ran deeper
into the forest until he came to a tiny cottage where
he saw another lady who might help him.

"Miss Witch, Miss Witch. Excuse me, Miss Witch.
I wonder if you could help me. I'm a prince and—"
"Eh? What did you say? Prince?" croaked the witch.

"No. I mean, yes. I mean, no, I'm not the prince looking
for Sleeping Beauty. But, yes, I'm the Frog Prince.
And I'm looking for a member of your profession who can
turn me back into a frog so I can live happily ever after."

"Frog Prince, you say? That's funny. I thought
frogs were little green guys with webbed feet.
Well, no matter. If you're a prince, you're a prince.
And I can't have any princes rescuing
Snow White. Here—eat the rest of this apple."

The Prince, who knew his fairy tales (and knew
a poisoned apple when he saw one), didn't
even stay to say, "No, thank you." He turned and
ran deeper into the forest. Soon he came
to a strange-looking house with a witch outside.

"*Ahem.* Miss Witch, Miss Witch. Excuse me, Miss Witch.
I wonder if you could help me? I'm the Frog—"
    "If you're a frog, I'm the King of France," said the witch.
    "No, I'm not a frog. I'm the Frog Prince. But
I need a witch to turn me back into a frog so I can

live happily ever after can you do it?" said the Prince
in one long breath.

The witch eyed the Prince and licked her rather plump lips.

"Why, of course, dearie. Come right in. Maybe I can
fit you in for lunch."

The Prince stopped on the slightly gummy steps.
Something about this house seemed very familiar.
He broke off a corner of the windowsill and tasted it.
Gingerbread.

"I hope you don't mind my asking, Miss Witch. But
do you happen to know any children by the
name of Hansel and Gretel?"

"Why yes, Prince darling, I do. I'm expecting them for dinner."

The Prince, who, as we said before, knew his fairy tales, ran as fast as he could deeper into the forest.

Soon he was completely lost.

He saw someone standing next to a tree.
The Prince walked up to her, hoping she wasn't
a witch, for he'd quite had his fill of witches.

"Madam. I am the Frog Prince. Could you
help me?"

"Gosh, do you need it," said the Fairy Godmother.
"You are the worst-looking frog I've ever seen."

"I am not a frog. I am the Frog Prince," said the Prince,
getting a little annoyed. "And I need someone
to turn me back into a frog so I can live happily ever after."

"Well, I'm on my way to see a girl in the village
about going to a ball, but I suppose I could give it a try.
I've never done frogs before, you know."

And with that the Fairy Godmother waved her magic
wand, and turned the Prince into a beautiful . . .

carriage.

The Prince couldn't believe his rotten luck.

The sun went down. The forest got spookier.
And the Prince became more and more frightened.

h, what an idiot I've been. I could be sitting at home with the Princess, living happily ever after. But instead, I'm stuck here in the middle of this stupid forest, turned into a stupid carriage. Now I'll probably just rot and fall apart and live unhappily ever after."

The Prince thought these terrible, frightening kinds of thoughts (and a few worse— too awful to tell), until far away in the village, the clock struck midnight.

The Carriage instantly turned back into his
former Prince self, and ran by the light of the moon
until he was safe inside his own castle.

"Where have you been? I've been worried sick.
You're seven hours late. Your dinner is cold.
Your clothes are a mess."

The Prince looked at the Princess who had
believed him when no one else in the world had,
the Princess who had actually kissed his
slimy frog lips. The Princess who loved him.

The Prince kissed the Princess.
They both turned into frogs.
And they hopped off happily ever after.

The End.